Youn

STAR WARS®

FINN & THE FIRST ORDER

WRITTEN BY ELIZABETH SCHAEFER

ILLUSTRATED BY BRIAN ROOD

EGMONT

EGMONT

We bring stories to life

First published in Great Britain 2016
by Egmont UK Limited, The Yellow Building,
1 Nicholas Road, London W11 4AN.

© & TM 2016 Lucasfilm Ltd.

ISBN 978 1 4052 8364 9
64523/1
Printed in Singapore

To find more great *Star Wars* books, visit www.egmont.co.uk/starwars

This is Finn.

He is a stormtrooper.

Stormtroopers are soldiers
for the evil First Order.

One day, Finn and his team
were sent on a mission.

An old man had secret plans
that could hurt the First Order.

The man's name was Lor San Tekka.

The stormtroopers needed to find him.

The stormtroopers destroyed
the village where Lor was hiding.

Finn chose not to fire
at the people in the village.

Finn did not like being a stormtrooper.

Finn wanted to help people.

Lor gave the plans to a
Resistance pilot named Poe.

Poe knew he had to
keep the plans safe.

He gave them to his droid, BB-8.

'Get as far away from here as you can,'
Poe told BB-8.

A big shuttle landed on Jakku.

Inside was Kylo Ren,
a leader in the First Order.

Kylo told Lor to give him the secret plans.

Lor refused.

Kylo and the First Order captured Poe.

They took him back to their ship.

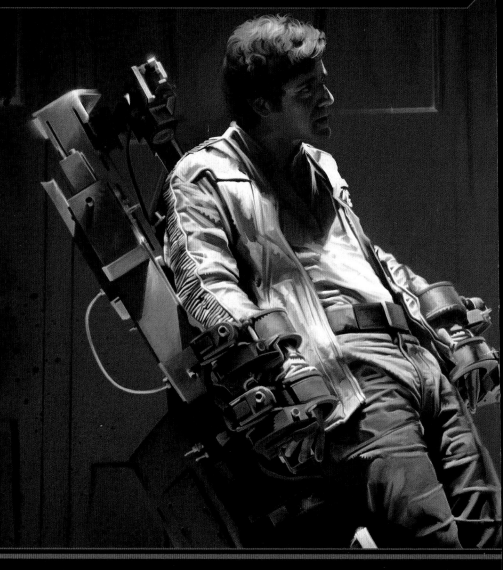

Kylo made Poe tell him
where the plans were.

Now the First Order
would hunt down BB-8.

Finn felt awful for
attacking the village.

The leader of his troop yelled
at him for not firing at the people.

Finn pretended his blaster
was broken.

Finn knew he didn't want to be a stormtrooper anymore.

It was too late to save the people in the village.

But he could still save Poe.

Finn went to Poe's cell and freed the Resistance pilot.

'Can you fly a TIE fighter?' Finn asked Poe.

'I can fly anything,' Poe replied.

Finn and Poe ran to the docking bay, where all the ships were kept.

They jumped into a TIE fighter and flew into space.

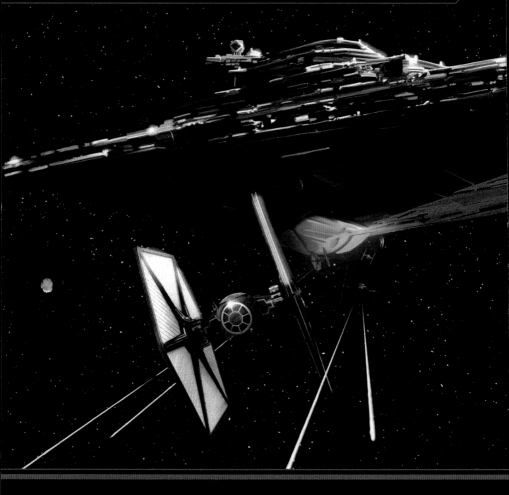

Poe flew the TIE fighter away from the First Order's ship.

Poe explained that he needed to find his droid, BB-8.

They had to go back to Jakku.

A blast from the First Order's ship hit Poe and Finn.

Their ship started spinning out of control.

They were going to crash on Jakku!

Finn pressed the eject button, and his seat flew out of the ship.

Finn landed on a sandy dune.

Nearby, the crashed TIE fighter began to sink into the sand.

Finn tried to find Poe,
but all he found was Poe's jacket.

Poe was gone.

Finn walked through the desert.

He was looking for a safe place
to stay.

Finn found a trading outpost.

He was shocked when
he saw Poe's droid, BB-8!

Thugs were trying to steal him.

A young woman named Rey
was trying to stop them.

The thugs weren't the only ones trying to take BB-8.

A team of stormtroopers arrived and fired at Rey and the droid.

Finn knew he had to help them.

Together, Finn, Rey and BB-8 ran from the stormtroopers.

It wasn't safe for them on Jakku.

They needed to find a ship
and fly away.

Rey led them to a shipyard.

They hopped on board an old ship.

The ship was called
the *Millennium Falcon*.

Rey flew the ship away from Jakku.

Finn fired at the enemy ships
to keep them from following.

Finn and Rey took BB-8 and the secret plans back to the Resistance.

Finn was finally free from the First Order!